FAERIEGROUND

The Seventh Kingdom

Book Ten

BY BETH BRACKEN AND KAY FRASER

ILLUSTRATED BY ODESSA SAWYER

STONE ARCH BOOKS
a capstone imprint

FAERIEGROUND IS PUBLISHED BY
STONE ARCH BOOKS
A CAPSTONE IMPRINT
1710 ROE CREST DRIVE
NORTH MANKATO, MINNESOTA 56003

WWW.CAPSTONEPUB.COM

LIBRARY OF CONGRESS CATALOGING-IN-PUBLICATION DATA

BRACKEN, BETH, AUTHOR.

  THE SEVENTH KINGDOM / BY BETH BRACKEN AND KAY FRASER ;
ILLUSTRATED BY ODESSA SAWYER.

    PAGES CM. -- (FAERIEGROUND ; [BK. 10])

  SUMMARY: SOLI IS STILL IN THE KINGDOM OF THE CROWS, WHO
WANT TO TURN HER INTO ONE OF THEM--MEANWHILE THE OTHER
SIX KINGDOMS ARE CHOOSING WHETHER TO UNITE AGAINST THE
CROWS, AND LUCY HAS LEARNED THAT HER OWN MOTHER, BACK
IN THE WORLD, COULD BRING RUIN IF SHE CROSSES OVER TO
FAERIEGROUND.

  ISBN 978-1-4342-9186-8 (LIBRARY BINDING) --- ISBN 978-1-4342-9190-5
(PBK.)

1. FAIRIES--JUVENILE FICTION. 2. BEST FRIENDS--JUVENILE FICTION.
3. MAGIC--JUVENILE FICTION. 4. SECRECY--JUVENILE FICTION.
5. CHOICE (PSYCHOLOGY)--JUVENILE FICTION. [1. FAIRIES--FICTION.
2. BEST FRIENDS--FICTION. 3. FRIENDSHIP--FICTION. 4. MAGIC--
FICTION. 5. SECRETS--FICTION. 6. CHOICE--FICTION.] 1. FRASER, KAY,
AUTHOR. II. SAWYER, ODESSA, ILLUSTRATOR. III. TITLE. IV. SERIES:
BRACKEN, BETH. FAERIEGROUND ; [BK. 10]

 PZ7.B6989SE 2014

 813.6--DC23

                              2013047442

BOOK DESIGN BY K. FRASER

ALL PHOTOS © SHUTTERSTOCK WITH THESE EXCEPTIONS: AUTHOR
PORTRAIT © K FRASER AND ILLUSTRATOR PORTRAIT © ODESSA
SAWYER

PRINTED IN CANADA.
032014
008086FRF14_FG

"Those who don't believe in magic
will never find it."

– Roald Dahl

For Etta, my daughter. — BB
To the love of my life and best friend JB — KF

Once, there were seven kingdoms.

But before that, there was one kingdom.

And it was a beautiful, happy place.

Chapter 1

Soli

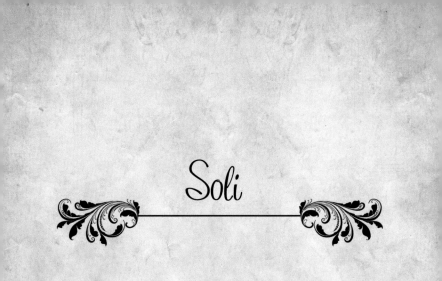

I lie back in bed.

Count the cracks in the plaster ceiling again, trying to pass time. Thirty-two of them today, same as yesterday. Same as every day.

I turn onto my stomach, and as I arrange the pillow under my head, something crackles beneath it.

Kheelan's letter. For the hundredth time, I read it.

Then I shove it back under the pillow and flip around onto my back. I imagine his hand on my cheek. His tender smile, his lips on mine.

I stare at the walls surrounding me, memorizing the tenderness of his words and gesture. He called me sweet. I can picture him saying it. Something inside my chest twists.

He wants to rescue me. They all do. Even people I've never met.

Not Lucy, though. I think she's making the right choice. Staying home, where she belongs. Where she's safe. She knows there is no chance here, or at least I think she must. She knows there is no hope for me.

The quest to rescue the captured Queen of Roseland is suicide, a far-fetched fairy tale. There is no way out of this place. Everyone knows that.

They can't save me.

"I'm a Crow," I whisper, testing the thought.

A knock on my door brings me back to my room. "Done moping? Ready to do some real work?" Caro asks, walking in. She's wearing boy clothes, and her sun-colored hair is up in a high ponytail.

"Anything to get out of this room," I say, standing up.

"Father thinks you'll turn lazy if you don't get exercise," she says, "so I convinced him to let you attend my classes."

I'm surprised by the light that glows inside me at the thought. "That is very kind of you," I say, and I mean it.

"Don't thank me yet," she says, grinning. "I don't think you know what you're getting yourself into."

She rummages through my drawers without asking and pulls out a pair of pants and a long-sleeved T-shirt. "Class will be tough in a dress," Caro says. "Put these on. And some boots."

"I don't have any boots," I say, looking around my tiny room, and she rolls her eyes.

"Back in a minute," she says. "I'll get you some of mine."

I dress quickly while she's gone. Caro doesn't care about privacy, so I know she won't knock when she comes back.

I'm just buttoning the pants when she throws my door open.

"Here," she says, tossing a pair of boots into my room. "Hurry up. Class starts in five minutes. If you're not on time, don't bother coming." She slams the door behind her.

I lace up the soft leather boots and look at the door. The handle has never moved for me before. I reach out and try it. I hear a click. The heavy door opens.

Chapter 2

Lucy

Kheelan is like a wild creature in the woods.

His wings seem to suspend him in the air
when he takes long strides. It's pretty amazing
to watch him. I try to not stare as we head
through the forest, but that gets harder and
harder the farther we go.

"Come on Lucy, keep up," Kheelan urges me.

"I'm not a faerie, you know. I'm a human girl,"
I call ahead to him.

He forgot I'm not Soli. He forgot I'm not one
of them. He forgot I'm an average teenage
girl.

"I'm sorry," he says, coming to a sudden stop. "I'm used to——"

"Soli," I say, finishing his sentence. "I know."

He nods, and his eyes become sad with the thought of her. I've never seen a boy so into a girl before. It seems real to him, as real and necessary as air is.

"Is she all right?" I ask. "Where is she?" I still don't know what happened, how I was sent home.

He kicks the dirt, and twigs lift from the ground. "Nothing has been all right."

Then he tells me. How the Crow king, Caro's father, asked Soli to choose between her true love and her best friend. And how, instead, she sent us both away.

"So that's why she didn't come to get me," I say.

He nods.

"Have you spoken to her?" I ask.

"No," he says, his face sad. "I've sent her letters. I have someone there who helps me."

"Who?" I ask, thinking of the Crow palace and the people I met there. I didn't meet anyone who didn't seem cruel. I certainly didn't meet anyone who would help Kheelan.

"I can't say," he says. "But I think the letters are getting there safely. Although I can't be sure. She hasn't written back. She's still with the Crows, as far as I know, but—it isn't safe for her to write."

I feel like crying when I think of the Crows. Chills run down my spine with each thought of black-feathered wings.

I don't feel brave enough to go back there.

Not yet.

"How do we get her out?" I ask.

Kheelan looks at me, and the beginnings of a smile start to spread across his face. "I'm working on it," he says. "Good thing you got here in time."

He is quiet for the rest of the walk, and I don't try to make conversation. I'm too busy thinking about my friend—my best friend, my almost-sister—trapped in the Crows' nest. I can only imagine Kheelan's frustration. Soli is not only the leader of Roseland, but she's also his true love.

It must be really hard for him, knowing she's out there.

After a while, he stops. "This way," he says, pushing aside a thatch of vines hiding a road.

The road to the palace is full of faeries. It is a colorful procession of soldiers bearing bright flags and banners.

And bows and arrows.

As we get closer, I begin to see tents scattered around the road. Six colors of tents, some clustered by color, some mixed together.

The faerieground has always been beautiful, but it's never been so colorful. Even the flowers seem to have bloomed while I've been gone.

The gloom that overcame this palace in the past is gone, destroyed.

"I wish Soli could see this," I say.

Kheelan nods. "Me too," he says. Then he grabs my hand and squeezes it. "I think she will. Soon."

I don't say anything in return.

I'm not sure he knows how powerful the Crows are.

"What are all these people doing here?" I ask, trying to understand.

"They are here for her," Kheelan says. "For the Queen of Roseland."

"Soli?" I ask.

He nods, solemn. "It's time for us to fight the Crows for her freedom."

"Fight as in, like, weapons?" I ask.

Kheelan nods. "Fight as in war."

Chapter 3

Soli

I hold the bow.

My right hand brushes my cheek, my left focuses on the target. Exhale, release.

My arrow flies true to the target for the third time in a row. Not quite a bull's-eye, but close enough. I can't help but grin.

"Good work, Soledad," the trainer says. "You're a natural."

Next to me, Caro snorts. She lifts her bow, aims, releases. Her arrow hits the bull's-eye for the third time. "You're good, but not that good," she mutters as the trainer walks away.

But I don't mind. Because of Caro, because she talked King Georg into letting me join her in classes, I've been out of my room for hours every day. Hand-to-Hand Combat. Archery. Etiquette. History. Faerie Dialects. Flora of the Human World. Botany.

I liked school, back in Mearston, but I never liked it this much. I'm nothing but thankful to Caro these days.

And lately I think I make a better Crow than I ever did a queen, or a daughter, or a friend, or a girlfriend.

I keep my stance, readying the arrow one last time. I close my eyes, letting my body take over without thinking.

My right hand brushes my cheek, and then I open my eyes, see the target, release.

My arrow slices through the air and breaks Caro's in half.

Someone claps. It startles both of us, and we whirl around.

Georg stands there. "Bravo, Soledad!" he says.

"Caro, you could learn a thing or two about poise from this one," he goes on. "I have no doubt that had it been a man instead of a target, Soledad would have made the shot just as easily."

Caro throws her bow down. "I would've killed faster than she ever could," she mutters, and then she walks away. I look at King Georg, who laughs as his daughter storms back toward the castle.

"You should not judge her so harshly," I say before I can stop myself.

The king raises his eyebrows, and Caro stops in her tracks.

"She is the sharpest archer I've seen in this castle," I say. "She has taught me everything I know. Anything I do right is because she has taught me right." I look down at my feet. But after a moment, it's still silent, so I raise my eyes to Georg's.

He nods. "Then I suppose congratulations are due to you both," he says. He bends his head in my direction and then walks away, brushing past his daughter. Caro smiles at me.

Chapter 4

Lucy

The throne room looks nothing
like I remember it.

The heavy draperies have been brushed back, letting light in, and the windows don't show a single crack. The room has been swept clean, and fresh-cut flowers line the surfaces.

Kheelan has brought me here. He and his father, Jonn, want to talk to me. I don't know what about. I guess it must be about the war they're planning.

"We are ready," Jonn says. A guard throws open the heavy double doors.

"What's happening?" I whisper.

But Kheelan and Jonn don't answer. They just stare, waiting, at the doors.

Then they come. Faeries march into the room. The only one I recognize is Motherbird. She sits beside me and reaches over to squeeze my hand.

Jonn clears his throat and stands. "Good morning, my friends," he says. His deep voice echoes in the large throne room. "And thank you for coming to Roseland on such short notice."

He looks around the table, and so do I. Besides Motherbird, who wears a red necklace, there is an older man with a yellow one; a woman who looks like she's my mom's age, wearing a violet one; a white-haired woman with an orange one; and a younger man whose necklace is indigo.

"Of course you will notice that two of the Seven are not here," Jonn goes on. "We sent a messenger to Georg, but heard no response."

"Did the messenger return?" mutters the older man with the yellow necklace.

Jonn shakes his head. "No, Lotham, he didn't."

"And Soledad, too, is gone," Motherbird says.

"Yes," Jonn says. "As you know, Queen Soledad has been a hostage of the Crows for a month."

"Now is the time," Jonn continues. He looks around the table, staring at each faerie in turn. "Now is the time," he says again.

Motherbird shifts next to me. "Now is the time," she says. But there's sadness in her voice, not fire, like in Jonn's.

I look at the other faeries. They stare at Jonn, not answering.

"The Crow kingdom has terrorized each of our own kingdoms for centuries," Jonn goes on.

"Calandra was the evil hcre," the white-haired woman says. "She almost ruined Roseland."

Jonn's nostrils flare. "Calandra—Queen Calandra—is not the point of discussion today," he says. "We have tried to deal with the Crows peacefully, but now, with Soledad—"

"Queen Soledad," Motherbird interrupts.

"Queen Soledad," Jonn says, nodding. "With Queen Soledad being held captive, we must take action."

"What happened, exactly?" the white-haired woman asks. But she doesn't ask Jonn. She's looking at Motherbird.

Motherbird smiles and closes her eyes. "Soledad was given a choice," she says. "She was told that she must choose between the boy, Kheelan, and her friend, Lucy. Georg wanted to make her vulnerable, so he told her to choose who would die."

"So who did Soledad choose?" asks the older man, Lotham.

"She chose herself," Motherbird says. "She used what little power she could pull away from Georg, and she sent Kheelan here and she sent Lucy home to Mearston." She pats my hand. "This is Lucy," she adds.

"Oh," the white-haired woman says. "Lucy is human." She wrinkles her nose at me.

"Indeed she is, Calla, and there's more to her than meets the eye," Motherbird says.

"But the point is, Soli didn't choose to stay there because she wanted to be there," Kheelan says. "Right, Motherbird?"

Motherbird nods. "That's right," she says. "She was asked to choose a person who would die by the hand of the Crows, and she chose herself."

A terror runs through me. "She's still alive, isn't she?" I whisper, and Motherbird squeezes my hand.

"Yes. She's still alive."

"War is not the answer," Lotham says. "War has never been the answer. War is what got us into this mess."

"Yes," says the younger man. "I understand that your queen is in need of rescue, but there must be some other way—"

"There is no other way, and there is no other time," says the other woman. "For far too long, the kingdom has been torn apart. For far too long, the Seven have been separate, and now is the time, and I know we all feel that."

The faeries look at each other. The younger man shakes his head. "Montan, what is your trouble with this?" Helenea asks.

"I do not like the idea of unity," Montan says. "My kingdom lives in peace, far away."

"But your brothers and sisters do not," Motherbird says, looking at him directly. "And if the Crows take us, they will soon take you."

"The unity of our kingdoms is our strength," Jonn says. "The numbers are in our favor. We can win if we are united."

"Let's vote," says Calla, and the other faeries nod.

"It is clear that I—and all of Roseland—vote for unity," Jonn says.

"As do I," says Lotham.

"And I," says Calla. She reaches up and rubs her orange necklace between her fingers.

"And I," says Helenea, "gladly." She smiles at Jonn, who looks surprised.

Montan is silent for a moment. He looks around the room, glancing over at the guards against the wall. "Fine," he says. "I vote for unity. But I pray we can keep our people safe."

"As do we all," Jonn says quietly. He turns to Motherbird. "You must vote," he says, his voice respectful.

But she turns to look at me. "Be ready," she says quietly.

I don't know what to say, so I just nod.

"The only way this allegiance will succeed," Motherbird says, turning her gaze to Jonn, "is if Andria does not cross over. If she returns to the faerieground, with her will come the end of us."

My jaw drops.

She can't possibly be talking about my mother.

Chapter 5

Soli

Another letter.

Sweet,

The light one has found her way to us, right in the nick of time. She's safe. And so am I. We're worried about you, of course. We fear for your life.

We know you're strong, but it's still hard to know you're there, all alone. I wish I was with you right now.

Motherbird told us today what happened, so now we know for sure how you chose to send Lucy and me home instead of choosing one of us to die.

I shouldn't be, but I'm grateful.

I wasn't ready to die then, especially by the Crows.

But I'm angry, too. I want to think that if you'd chosen to save her instead of me, I could have fought them, and I could have been safe.

And if you had chosen to save me, then we'd be together now.

But that chance is gone, and at least we're all alive.

The Six Kingdoms gathered today.

I won't tell you our decisions, because I don't know who might come across this letter, but I'll tell you I feel strong and brave.

You are in my mind, and in the light one's, and in the minds of all the faeries in your kingdom and beyond.

I know in my heart we are meant to be, Sweet. We are meant to be real, and to grow old together——if not this time, maybe next.

I will hold you in my heart until then.

I will hold you in my heart always.

yours—

K

Chapter 6

Soli

The words on the paper turn blurry.

My hands begin to shake. I can't sit still, so I stand. I'm allowed to leave my room these days, so I take advantage of it.

As I walk down the hallways, I hold my mother's key in my hand, like every time I'm tense these days. The feeling of the cold metal digging into my skin makes me feel better.

I can't stop thinking about the letter. I do not need rescuing; I do not need them to risk their lives. The lives of everyone in the kingdom. I chose to stay here to save them, not put them all in more danger. I have accepted my fate.

My fate is to become a Crow.

At the end of this hallway, there's a little nook, tucked away beneath a staircase. I fold my body inside.

Tears roll down my cheeks. When I reach up to wipe them away, the key clatters to the ground.

There is a tile mosaic inlaid in the floor in this nook. It's shaped like a bird—a crow, of course, mouth open in a caw. I trace it with my finger. The tiles are cold, smooth to the touch.

Then I see it. In the bird's gaping mouth, a tiny keyhole.

I scramble to my knees, pick up the key, and slide it into the hole. Then I turn it. It clicks. And the wall in front of me begins to move.

Once the wall is gone, there's a long, dark hallway. It's deathly silent. But I'm not afraid. I want to see where my mother's key leads me.

After I walk through, the wall slides up behind me again. I walk down the damp hallway. My boots slide across the cement floor.

The cracks around the hidden entrance let in enough light to see by for a while. But after I've walked for a minute, it becomes too dark. I have to reach out my hands and touch the walls so that I can guide myself down the hall.

I find myself in a room lit by tiny flames in glass bowls against the wall. It's some kind of library. The room is lined with shelves of books.

The room is undeniably creepy, and I know I'm not supposed to be here. I know if Georg found out, he'd be furious.

If he even knows it's here. Caro has never mentioned it. But then again, Caro doesn't really like books.

Against one wall, there's an old wooden desk covered with books. Some are open, some are closed. Next to the desk, there's a pile of seven rolled-up papers. I pick one and unroll it. It's a map of a kingdom; not the Crows', and not my own.

I try another one. In fancy writing across the top: *Roseland*.

I've never seen the shape of my kingdom

before. It isn't shaped like a rose, of course.

It's more like a diamond. I think it must be the

kingdom most central in the faerieground. It's

bordered by the Crows' kingdom on one side,

and the Ladybirds' on the other.

But then I look closer. Tight black writing on

the map marks places where the Crows can

enter without being stopped by guards, places

that they can burn to the ground, places they

can attack in the night.

I throw the map aside and look at the others.

All of them are the same. A detailed map, with notes on how to kill as many as possible.

The Crows plan to murder everyone. They plan to bring war across the faerieground. And if I have become a Crow, then I'm as bad as they are.

A book on the desk catches my eye. It is a black leather-bound book, heavy, with thin pages. I open it to a random page and instantly find my name. *Soledad trained for most of the morning today; she holds a bow well and sinks arrows deep.*

I flip earlier in the book, find another page.

Magnus deceased; poison was effective. The halfling princess is too young to know, of course.

A bit later: *Calandra has lost control of her kingdom. The faeries believe she killed Magnus.*

On the next page: *The Old Ones have taken the child and given her to Andria for safekeeping. The spell blocking their knowledge of Andria will fade, but it worked well enough. Our Queen will send the child back when she's old enough to lead; we will find her and make her one of our own. Now we wait.*

I read more, and find this: *The halfling princess has returned. She is with the daughter of Andria. The pieces of our old plan have fallen into place perfectly.*

The Crows planned this all along. They took me from Calandra. They tricked the Ladybirds into bringing me to Andria.

As far as I can tell, their plan was this: Kill my father. Turn Roseland against my mother. Steal me away. Make my mother crazy. Bring me back and steal me again. Make me a Crow. Attack Roseland. Attack the other kingdoms. Kill everyone who stands in their way.

Chapter 7

Lucy

"They can't be talking about my mom," I whisper to Kheelan.

"She can be weird sometimes, but she wouldn't do whatever it is they think she'd do."

We are crouching outside the clinic where my mother works.

Kheelan shakes his head. "Motherbird is never wrong," he says. "Maybe you just haven't seen that side of your mother."

"It just doesn't make sense!" I say. "I know she was in the faerieground, and I know something weird happened there. But I also know she would never go back. I mean . . ."

I trail off, thinking about how my mother told us never to go into the woods, how she left offerings for the faeries, how she told me she'd angered the queen.

"We need to figure out why Motherbird thinks she's a danger," Kheelan says. "She wouldn't tell us, but I could tell the other leaders knew something."

I nod. "They all looked at each other and gave me weird looks when they found out I'm her daughter," I admit. "I just don't get it."

Kheelan checks the sky. The sun is sinking lower. "When will she be done?" he asks.

"Any time now," I say. And just like that, the automatic doors slide open and my mother walks out.

She turns onto the sidewalk, and after she's walked halfway down the block, Kheelan and I get up and follow her. But she doesn't turn toward home at the end of the street. Instead, she walks further into town. We follow her all the way to the Mearston Historical Society.

She goes in, and we creep close to the door.

I can see her through the window. "She looks bad," I say. "Tired. Maybe she's just been worried about me. Since I disappeared two days ago."

"Maybe," he says.

We hear loud voices coming from inside. My mother is yelling at someone I can't see. "How could you?" she screams. The other person replies, but I can't make out the words.

"Do you know the woman she's talking to?" Kheelan asks, leaning closer to the window.

I peer inside. "It's Molly Murry," I say. "She works here. She's the one who helped me. She knew about my necklace." My knees shake. "Molly knows how to cross to the faerieground," I say.

Then we hear Molly yell, "Fine! I'll help you!"

Kheelan takes my hand and pulls me into a run. We hurry toward the woods. Tears stream down my face. Motherbird was right.

Chapter 8

Soli

If I need to send a message, how can I send it?

Messages are coming to me, but I don't know how they get here. And I can't talk to anyone about them.

I don't know who I can ask. Certainly not the king; that would be stupid. Not any of the teachers. Not Caro.

There's not one person here I can trust, not really. I suppose I knew that already.

I toss and turn all night, trying to figure out what to do. How to warn the people I love, the people I'm responsible for in Roseland.

Because that's the truth, isn't it? I'm still

responsible for them. I'm still the queen.

But then I realize something. Someone here

in the Crows' palace is working against the

Crows. Someone is bringing me the letters,

even though they shouldn't. Someone is

betraying their own kingdom by helping

Kheelan's messages come to me. That person,

whoever it is, is my only hope.

Otherwise, the Crows will kill me, and then

they'll take over the whole faerieground.

I finally doze off just as the sun is rising outside my small window. But a knock wakes me up. Caro walks in. She narrows her eyes as soon as she sees me. "You look terrible," she says.

I'm used to her bluntness. "I know," I say. "I couldn't sleep." I don't want to tell her why.

"What's wrong?" she asks.

I shake my head. "Just homesick, I guess," I say. And it's true. Sometimes this whole adventure feels like a nightmare I can't wake up from.

Caro nods. "It must be hard, all the changes in your life," she says. "Two months ago, you didn't even know we existed."

She's right. "Yes," I say. "It's been hard. Parts have been wonderful. But——" I can't say any more.

She smiles. "There's a place I go," she says, cocking her head. "When I need to get away from everyone else, when my father is being awful, you know. I think it could help you. Would you like to see it?"

Her face is relaxed, and I'm surprised by how much I like her right now, the daughter of my captor.

"Okay," I say. "But won't we be late for class?"

She shrugs. "I miss classes all the time. If you're going to fit in around here, you might as well miss one too."

That makes me laugh.

"Let's go," she says.

"I should dress," I say, but she shakes her head.

"Don't bother."

She takes my hand and guides me through the castle. We head up a narrow staircase, step after step, up past four or five landings. Finally, at the top, there's a small wooden door.

"Ready?" she asks. She bites her lip, and it strikes me that she's nervous.

"Does anyone else know about this place?" I ask.

She shrugs. "It must be on the castle maps," she says. "I'm sure someone knows about it. But no one ever comes here. You're the first person I've ever told about it."

Then she opens the door. A cool breeze comes through the wide-open windows that line each wall. The room is full of potted plants and flowers, varieties I've never seen before mixed with familiar roses and lilies.

"This is beautiful," I say, dropping down to a wood bench near the door.

"This is where I come when I need to think, when I need some time alone." Caro says.

"I can see why," I say. I gaze out the window. The tower's height lets me see the valley the castle is built in and the grounds around it. "This is really beautiful."

She smiles. "I'm glad you like it," she says.

And I do. But as I stare out at the amazing view, I remember that this beautiful place, and everything in it, was built by faeries who want to destroy the rest of the kingdoms.

"Your face changed," Caro says. "What are you thinking about?"

"Just thinking about home," I say.

"Would you believe I've never crossed over to the human world?" she asks. She laughs. "I've been in prisons in all seven faerie kingdoms, but I've never even seen a human home." Then she says, "What's it like, where you're from?"

I think about Mearston. "It's just home," I say. "It's hard to describe. I've lived there all my life—"

"Since you were two, anyway," she puts in.

"Right," I say. "Since I've had memories, anyway. It's a small town, not many buildings, not many people. I didn't have many friends, besides Lucy. We did everything together. She's like a sister to me."

"You must miss her," Caro says. And she reaches over and pats my hand. "I hope you'll see her soon."

"Me too," I whisper, and a tear slides down my cheek.

"Didn't you ever want to leave your human world?" Caro asks.

I shake my head. "I just wanted to be with Lucy," I say. "I didn't care where I was, as long as my best friend was with me."

"Now you don't have Lucy, and you don't have Kheelan," she says. "You must feel so alone."

"I do," I say. "But you've been nice to me."

"It's nice for me, too," she says. "To not be alone here."

Caro crosses to the windows and looks out. "I'm the king's daughter. There are no friends here for me." She looks back at me, and a spark flashes in her eyes. "Except you."

She waits for me to respond, but I don't know what to say.

Do I feel like Caro is a friend?

Yes, I do.

Do I feel like Caro is someone I trust?

I still don't know.

"We should go," I say finally. "I don't mind missing one class, but two is too many. They'll look for me."

Caro sighs, and we leave, and she locks the door behind her.

Whether I am a Crow or not, at least I'm not completely alone.

Now I just have to wait until my people come for me. And hope they survive.

Beth & Kay

Kay Fraser and *Beth Bracken* are a designer-editor team in Minnesota.

Kay is from Buenos Aires. She left home at eighteen and moved to North Dakota—basically the exact opposite of Argentina. These days, she designs books, writes, makes tea for her husband, and drives their daughters to their dance lessons.

Beth and her husband live in a light-filled house with their son, Sam, and their daughter, Etta. Beth spends her time editing, reading, daydreaming, and rearranging her furniture.

Kay and Beth both love dark chocolate, Buffy, and tea.

Odessa

Odessa Sawyer is an illustrator from Santa Fe, New Mexico. She works mainly in digital mixed media, utilizing digital painting, photography, and traditional pen and ink.

Odessa's work has graced the book covers of many top publishing houses, and she has also done work for various film and television projects, posters, and album covers.

Highly influenced by fantasy, fairy tales, fashion, and classic horror, Odessa's work celebrates a whimsical, dreamy and vibrant quality.